CORAL'S REEF

Other Avon Books by
Dee Scarr

TOUCH THE SEA

DEE SCARR grew up in South Florida and taught high
school English, public speaking, and debate before taking
up scuba diving and eventually becoming a full-time dive
guide on San Salvador in the Bahamas. In 1980 she moved
to Bonaire in the Netherlands Antilles, and in 1982 she created *Touch the Sea,* a program of personalized dive guiding
to help other divers experience the gentle sea. She has pre-
sented *Touch the Sea: The Slide Experience* to school
groups, dive clubs, and underwater symposia, and has writ-
ten articles for several magazines, including *Skin Diver, Sea
Frontiers, Undersea Naturalist,* and *Diving and Snorkeling.*

Her first book, *Touch the Sea,* was published in 1984.
Coral's Reef is her first book for young readers.

CORAL'S REEF

Dee Scarr

Illustrated by Heleen Cornet

AN AVON CAMELOT BOOK

AVON BOOKS
A division of
The Hearst Corporation
1790 Broadway
New York, New York 10019

First Camelot Printing, November 1985

CAMELOT TRADEMARK REG. U. S. PAT. OFF. AND IN
OTHER COUNTRIES, MARCA REGISTRADA, HECHO EN
U. S. A.

Printed in the U. S. A.

OPM 10 9 8 7 6 5 4 3 2

DEDICATION: I would like to dedicate this book to children everywhere and to all the creatures of the seas in the hope that they will grow to understand and appreciate one another.

WITH GRATITUDE TO all those people who took the time to read my manuscript and offer invaluable suggestions. The children: first and foremost, Stephanie Ruza (who happily grants me access to her library), Brian Glover, and Brian Bongiorno. The adults (listed alphabetically since that's a grown-up thing to do): Marilyn Abramson, Judy Albert, Lee Bona, Donna and Dick Eisley, Dr. Alan Emery, Diane Matza, Karen Pearson, and Kathy van Amburg. A special thanks goes to Ellen Krieger, the editor of this book; to Heleen Cornet, the illustrator (who skillfully provided biologically accurate illustrations); and to Oliver Twist, the peacock flounder in whose memory Oliver Octopus was named.

I am fortunate to live on Bonaire. The totally protected marine environment here, the easily-accessible reefs, and the wonderful people have surely helped my ideas to develop. The encouragement of Captain Don Stewart of Captain Don's Habitat and Niki Tromp of the Bonaire Government Tourist Bureau, is very precious.

FOREWORD: The sea is an incredibly special place to me, a place of gentle interactions, yet it is often portrayed by the media as a place of danger. Those most hurt by this inaccuracy are children, whose fear of the sea deprives them of the opportunity to appreciate its magic.

It's very important to me that you understand that every behavior and every interaction that Coral and Tommy observe and participate in—with the sole exception of their discussions with Oliver—is a behavior or an interaction that I have personally observed or experienced. I can't emphasize this enough; the sea portrayed in this book is the sea I know.

Now, about that sole exception: I am warned that a talking octopus will place *Coral's Reef* in the realm of fantasy; that since no talking octopus has been dissected and categorized by the scientists, it is not possible that one exists.

But think for a moment: if you were Oliver, would *you* reveal yourself to a person wielding a test tube or a scalpel? Neither would I! And it is only recently that biologists have begun to recognize the study of animal behavior as legitimate. Who knows what they'll discover now?

As you settle down to read about the discoveries Coral and Tommy make in the gentle sea, please excuse me—it's time for me to go diving.

1 Coral's Challenge

Sharks! That was all Coral could think of as she and Linda cleaned their masks and rinsed them. Coral had never even seen the ocean before she'd arrived on the island of Bonaire yesterday, and now she had a chance to go snorkeling and see the animals beneath it. Her dad had shown her how to use the mask, fins, and snorkel in the YMCA pool at home; now Linda would take her into the real ocean near the hotel.

"Um, Linda, have you ever seen a shark?" Coral asked.

"Sure, lots of 'em! In *Jaws*, and *Jaws II*, and *The Deep*, and specials on TV. But don't worry about sharks here, Corrie. Just put your face in the water and you'll forget about everything except what you're seeing."

Coral did.

Wow! It was like floating on top of an aquarium. Colorful fish swam everywhere, in between branching corals and rocks and even around each other. Linda waved for Coral to join her, and Coral lifted her feet off the bottom, kicked her fins, and followed. Using the snorkel tube as she'd learned, she didn't even have to lift her face from the water to breathe. Seeing the real reef was even more exciting than her parents' books had promised.

Coral forgot about sharks.

After a swim around the reef, Linda led the way to a rock shelf and pointed at a pile of pebbles and shells near an old tin

can. The water was so shallow that they could stand up and talk.

"That's an octopus's den down there, Corrie," Linda explained. "Octopuses are very shy and it probably won't come out, but I've brought some fish to try to tempt it. Watch."

They put their faces in the water and Linda held a piece of fish near the den. Now that she knew what to look for, Coral could see one arm of the octopus with its two rows of round suckers. Suddenly the octopus moved closer to the opening of its den and they could see one of its eyes peering out at Linda's hand. An arm reached out, curled around the piece of fish, and pulled the fish into the den under the octopus's body.

"He's close enough to the entrance to touch, Corrie. Watch me, and then you do it."

Linda reached down and touched the octopus's arm. The animal changed colors—from gray to red and then back to gray—but held still. Linda moved away and motioned for Coral to try.

10

Coral had never touched an octopus before. As a matter of fact, she'd never touched *any* sea creature before. But if Linda had done it, it must be okay. . . . Slowly, Coral extended her hand and touched the octopus. How smooth it was! As Coral touched one of its arms, the octopus reached out with another arm and began to explore Coral's hand. Surprised, she jumped a little at first, but then kept her hand still. Then the octopus grasped her hand with several of its arms and pulled hard. Coral gasped. Then, suddenly, it let go.

"Linda, why did he do that?"

"I'm not positive . . . but see how the entrance to his den is blocked by lots of rocks and stuff? I think he wanted to see if he could use your hand to hide his den, too. When you pulled back he must have realized it wouldn't work."

"Aw, c'mon, Linda, can you really tell what an octopus is thinking?"

"I can't be sure, of course. But I like octopuses so I watch

11

them a lot. The more I watch them, the better I feel I understand them. It seems to me that that's a logical reason for an octopus to grab your hand. Now," she continued, "I see the dive boat returning. Let's go meet your folks!"

That night at dinner, as she told her parents about Linda and the octopus, Coral got an idea. She would snorkel every day they were on Bonaire. Maybe she, too, could watch animals like Linda did, and learn to think like them. What would it be like to be a fish living on a coral reef? Or an octopus with eight arms? Now she had a chance to find out!

There was only one problem Coral hadn't thought about: she wasn't allowed to snorkel alone. So the next morning while her parents were out diving and Linda was teaching a scuba class, Coral found herself wandering around, snorkeling gear in hand, wishing for someone to snorkel with. What a silly problem to hold up her plan!

At the pool she saw a boy, also with mask, fins, and snorkel, looking sadly toward the sea.

"Hi! You don't look very happy," Coral said to him. "Didn't I see you on the dive boat yesterday?"

"Yes, I went out snorkeling on the scuba boat, and it was terrific! I could see the divers below me, and I brought some bread and fed the fish. A great big scrawled filefish took bread right from my hands—you should see the weird puckered-up mouths those guys have! And the guide told me they hardly ever take food from people's hands!" the boy exclaimed, all in a rush. "But today the boat went to a deeper reef, and they told me I wouldn't see very much. So here I am, stuck at the pool, because I'm not allowed to go snorkeling alone!"

"Me neither. D'you think it'd be okay for us to snorkel together?"

"That would be great! But we'd better wait until we ask. . . . What's your name?"

"I'm Coral."

"Coral? Like a coral head? I never heard of anyone named Coral before."

"Well, my parents really like diving and the coral reef and all, so they thought they'd name me after it. Kids laugh at my name a lot, 'cause it's different, I guess, but you're the first one who knew what it meant."

"Oh, gee, I wasn't laughing. I think it's a great name. But you're right—it sure is different! I'm Tommy."

"It's nice to meet you, Tommy," Coral said, remembering her manners. "You can call me 'Corrie' if you want to. That's what most people do."

"Oh, okay Corrie. And I'm glad to meet you, too, especially if that means I don't have to sit around on shore all day!"

"While you were out on the boat yesterday, Linda and I were snorkeling right out here. We went all around the reef and she showed me an octopus, and she even fed him a piece of fish. Then I touched him—he felt real smooth—and he grabbed my hand!"

"Really? What did you do?"

"I jumped at first. Then I held still and he let me go. Linda thinks he wanted my hand to guard his house."

"To guard his house? Why'd she think that?"

"Well, he had a bunch of other stuff out there—rocks and shells and even a tin can. You know what? I'll bet I could find his house again—I could show it to you if we can snorkel this afternoon."

"That would be neat!"

"And Linda showed me a big coral head, with an anemone on top and a moray eel living underneath it. The anemone was pretty; it looked a lot like a flower. Have you ever snorkeled out front?"

"Nah. I've been going out on the boat."

"It's really super out there!"

"Um, well, I never had anyone to buddy with except on the boat. I'd like to see the reef out front. I've seen anemones be-

14

fore, but never a moray eel or an octopus. Hey, look—here comes the boat.''

Coral and Tommy ran to the dock to meet their parents.

"Mom! Dad! Can I go snorkeling out here if I have a buddy?" Tommy asked.

"Depends on the buddy, Tom," his father replied.

"It's Corrie," Tommy pointed her out, talking to her parents nearby. "She was snorkeling out front with Linda yesterday. She knows where there's an octopus!"

"Oh, we met Corrie's parents on the boat today," Tommy's mother said. "We were thinking you two might want to come out on the boat this afternoon."

"But the octopus . . ."

"Tell you what, Tom. Why don't we have lunch with Corrie and her parents and we'll talk about it?" Tommy's father suggested.

At lunch, Coral's father came up with a plan everyone liked: the children could snorkel together—without an adult—as long as they stayed between the hotel's two docks. The perfect plan, especially since the octopus's den was in that area!

2 An Underwater Friend

That afternoon, Coral and Tommy got some fish from Linda and snorkeled out to the octopus's den. Coral held out the fish, and, just as it did with Linda, the octopus reached out one arm, wrapped it around the fish, and pulled the fish into its den. Then Coral heard, ''Thank you.''

''Tommy!'' she cried, standing up. ''Did you just say 'Thank you?' ''

"No—I thought *you* said it!"

Coral and Tommy looked at each other, then flopped back into the water. The octopus had moved to just outside the entrance of its den. "*I* was the one who said 'Thank you,' " they heard, and one of the octopus's arms pointed at his body. "It wouldn't be very polite for me to take your gift without thanking you, would it?"

"But . . . but . . . Linda never told me you could *talk!*" Coral found herself saying, right into her snorkel.

"Well, obviously I *can* talk, because I *am* talking! I used to try to talk to humans, but they never heard me, so I gave up. Today I just thanked you automatically—I'm as surprised that you heard me as you seem to be that I'm talking!" The octopus bobbed his body up and down as he gave his little speech, looking at Coral with one eye and Tommy with the other.

Coral didn't want the octopus to think that she and Tommy were rude. "My name is Coral, and this is Tommy. We're thrilled to be able to talk with you. Would you mind if we visited you? We'll only be on Bonaire for a few days, so we won't bother you for long. And we'll bring you more fish."

The octopus bobbed again. "I'll be glad to have you come by to talk with me; sometimes I get awfully lonely. And you don't have to bring me food, you know. I can get my own. What I'll really enjoy is your company."

"How?" Tommy asked.

"How will I enjoy your company?"

"No, how do you get food?"

"Oh. Well, do you see all these shells around my house? Once or twice a day, usually at night or at sunrise or sunset, I leave my house to explore the reef and hunt. When I find a shell, I bring it home. Then I eat the animal that lives inside."

"But how do you do that?" Coral asked. "When I pick up a live shell, the animal goes inside and all I see is that hard thing at the entrance to the shell."

"That hard thing, Coral, is called the operculum," the octo-

17

pus informed them, bobbing up and down with importance as he explained. "The animal uses it as a trap door, to block the opening of its shell. Most of the time when I get a shell I wait for the animal to come out. But if I'm really hungry, I attach my suckers to the operculum and pull. Usually I'm stronger than the animal. The trap door might work most of the time, but not against an octopus!"

"Why do you leave the shells outside your house?"

"Oh, for a lot of reasons. They help to block off my doorway and protect me. Sometimes hermit crabs come to live in the shells, and once in a while I like to have a hermit crab for a snack. And the shells make nice decorations, don't you think?"

"They sure do. They're so pretty!"

"I, um, seem to have quite a few at my doorstep these days. If you children would like to take one apiece—only one apiece, mind you; no need to be greedy—you may do so," the octopus proclaimed, bobbing up and down.

"Thank you!" said Coral.

"Thank you!" said Tommy. "We'll bring you some fish tomorrow."

"Well, as I said before," the octopus bobbed, "the fish is not necessary. Not that I don't like it, you understand. It *is* rather nice for a change. I don't catch many fish. But what I really enjoy is your company. See you tomorrow!"

"Goodbye! C'mon, Tommy, I'll show you the coral head that Linda showed me yesterday."

The children tucked the shells into their bathing suits, waved to the octopus, and swam off. Soon they were above the coral head. There was the anemone, right on top. Its arms waved around in the current. Coral noticed something she hadn't seen yesterday: "Look, Tommy, there's something inside the anemone!"

They looked more closely. "It's a shrimp, I think. I can see white whiskers and a tiny body. I wonder if I can lift it out of

18

the anemone so we can see it better." Tommy reached for the shrimp. When his hand touched the tentacles of the anemone, he jerked it back. "It grabbed me!"

"Did it hurt?"

"No-o-o. It felt weird, though. You try it."

Coral lowered her hand to the anemone and touched one tentacle with her finger. The tentacle stuck to her finger. She touched it with another finger, and a tentacle stuck to that one, too. Coral wriggled her hand, and the tentacles let go. Then she couldn't get any of them to stick to her hand at all. "Gee, Tommy, at first it stuck to my finger but now it won't. It feels . . . really smooth. Like silk."

"Maybe we can get that shrimp out now."

Coral had been so interested in touching the anemone that she'd forgotten about the shrimp. Now she found it again, way down near the bottoms of the tentacles. She reached down with her fingers spread and placed them near the shrimp. Then she moved her fingers together. The shrimp jumped onto her hand, and scurried around as she lifted it closer to the surface. The little animal was barely as big as Coral's thumbnail, and its white whiskers were longer than its body. The reason it had been so hard to see was that it was almost transparent. It did have a little color, though, a bluish-purple stripe along each side of its body.

"It doesn't seem scared at all," Tommy noticed as they watched it.

Coral thought about Linda, and tried to think like the shrimp might think. "My fingers look a little like anemone tentacles," she thought out loud. "Maybe the shrimp just thinks it's in another, strange anemone?"

The shrimp, wandering around Coral's hand, came to a cut on one of her fingers. It began to pull dead skin from the cut. "Ouch!" she cried. "What's it doing *that* for?"

"Hey, did you ever hear of cleaner shrimp?" Tommy asked. "They live in anemones, and I remember now that fish

19

come to the anemones so that the shrimp can clean stuff off their bodies. I'll bet we've found a cleaner shrimp! What does it feel like?''

"At first it felt like almost nothing . . . like an ant feels when it's running around your hand. But now that it's playing with that cut, it hurts! I think I'll put it back into its anemone.''

"Corrie, do you think that if we were farther away from the anemone and the cleaner shrimp, we might see a fish get cleaned? Maybe we're so close we're scaring away the customers.''

"Good idea, Tommy. Let's try it.''

They drifted a few feet away, then waited. The longer they floated without moving, the more fish they saw, swimming around the coral head and in and out of the branched corals nearby. They watched quietly. Soon a brown fish with tiny blue spots—a coney, they found out later—swam up near the anemone. First one shrimp, then another and another glided out of the anemone and onto the fish. Carefully, Coral and Tommy swam in just close enough to see the almost-invisible shrimp moving along the coney's body. One shrimp worked on the fish's eye, using its tiny claws to pluck off creatures too small for the children to see. The coney opened its mouth, and two other shrimp scurried inside.

Do the shrimp want that fish to eat them? Coral wondered. Should she do something? She didn't want the shrimp to be eaten! Finally she decided it would be better to watch; she wouldn't always be around to protect the shrimp.

At first the shrimp worked where Coral and Tommy could see them, right at the edge of the coney's mouth. They were cleaning the fish's teeth! Then the coney flared out his cheeks—his gills—and the shrimp moved farther inside his mouth and down his throat until they were out of sight. Coral wondered again if they would be the fish's dinner. But after a little while, one shrimp popped back out of the fish's mouth. Where was the other one? Soon it walked right out of the fish's gill opening! The coney closed its mouth and shook its body, the three shrimp returned to the anemone, and the fish swam off.

"Oh, Tommy, what a neat way to be cleaned! I wonder if octopuses get cleaned too? Or maybe they clean themselves, since they have so many arms! Do you think our friend would climb up near an anemone? Do you—do you realize we never asked him his name?''

"That will be the first thing we ask him tomorrow! Hey—here come the dive boats! I can't wait to tell my folks what we've seen—and heard! A talking octopus! Imagine that!"

"That'll be a problem, I bet," muttered Coral as they climbed up onto the dock. "They'll never, never believe us. They'll say we imagined it."

Tommy's grin faded. "You're right. They'll maybe pretend to believe us, while they say to each other 'Aren't they cute? What imaginations!' "

"Maybe we should leave out the part about the octopus talking."

"Yeah. They'll understand everything else okay."

Agreed on their secret, the children ran to meet their parents.

3 Discoveries

The next morning, as soon as their parents left to go diving, Coral and Tommy snorkeled out to the octopus's house. "Hi Coral! Hi Tommy! Isn't it a beautiful day?" their new friend greeted them.

"Oh yes, Mr. . . . uh . . ." Coral began. "Gee, we don't even know what to call you!"

"How about 'Oliver?' " the octopus asked. "I've always liked the sound of that: Oliver Octopus." He bobbed up and down.

"Oliver Octopus," Tommy tried, into his snorkel. "It comes out funny!"

"Well, some words *do* sound strange when you have to say them through a snorkel, I suppose." Oliver seemed hurt.

"We wish we could speak directly into the water like you do, Oliver," Coral said, wanting to make Oliver feel better. "Oliver's a lovely name!"

"The water's really clear this morning, Oliver," Tommy noted. It was true, but he also wanted to change the subject. "What's that long skinny fish over there doing?"

"Ah, you mean the trumpetfish, Tommy." Asked for help, Oliver seemed his old self. He bobbed up and down in his doorway. "Why don't you watch him for a while and see if you can figure it out?"

"Good idea!" said Coral. Talking to Oliver was terrific, but she still wanted to learn some things by herself.

"We'll be back soon, Oliver!" Tommy cried, and off they went.

The trumpetfish Tommy had seen was the longest, skinniest fish around. He was as long as Tommy's arm, but would have been able to swim through the "O" Tommy could make with his thumb and forefinger. The trumpetfish's head was a bright golden yellow which faded to light brown behind his eyes. His mouth was at the very tip of his body, at the end of a jaw that extended three inches in front of his eyes. When Coral and Tommy first swam over him, he was floating head down within the swaying arms of a flexible coral tree, and except for his bright colors would have been perfectly hidden. As the children watched, a blue-and-green fish that Coral recognized as a parrotfish swam by the soft coral, and the trumpetfish began to swim just above the parrotfish, almost touching its body, curving his own body to fit around the curve of the parrotfish's body. *Why in the world is he doing that?* Coral wondered, and remembering Linda's advice, she watched quietly.

The parrotfish cruised around the bottom, nibbling with its beaklike mouth on coral heads and rocks, leaving scrape marks at each place it tasted. With its bright colors and beak, it was easy to see why it was called a parrotfish! Smaller fish paid no attention to the parrotfish; Coral guessed they weren't afraid of it, since it didn't seem to eat fish. As the parrotfish nibbled, the trumpetfish stayed close. Then he began to sway his head back and forth, back and forth. Suddenly he darted at a little white fish that blended in with the bottom so well that Coral hadn't even seen it. The white fish dashed under a rock, and the trumpetfish backed away, only to realize that the parrotfish was gone. The trumpetfish seemed to look around, as if trying to decide what to do next.

Up at the surface, Tommy pointed behind them at a large

24

school of bright blue fish called blue tangs. All at once the school stopped swimming as the tangs mobbed a rock, nibbling at the algae growing on it. Little brown fish darted out, nipping at the tangs. The nipped ones swam off, but there were so many fish in the mob that the brown fish just couldn't chase them all away no matter how frantically they nipped. The school of tangs finished with the rock and rushed on, stopping now and then to mob another rock or the bases of the branchy corals.

As the school passed beneath Coral and Tommy, the trumpetfish joined it, swimming along within the mass of blue fish. They stopped again to mob a rock. More of the brown fish concentrated on nipping the blue tangs. The trumpetfish began to sway his head again, then suddenly shot forward at one of the small brown fish. In a flash the trumpetfish's mouth opened as wide as his body was thick, and the little brown fish was swallowed! Through the skin on the trumpetfish's jaw, Coral and Tommy could see the brown fish struggling. The trumpetfish slowly opened his mouth wide again, and then again; the brown fish was moved along the jaw farther into the trumpetfish's body until they couldn't see it any more. The trumpetfish glided over to a flexible coral, turned head down, and hovered within the branches of the coral, just as he had when Tommy had first seen him. The school of blue tangs continued along the reef.

Tommy's head popped out of the water. "Did you see *that*?"

"I saw the trumpetfish *eat* that little brown fish! Is that what you saw, Tommy?"

"Yes! The brown fish was a damselfish, wasn't it? Gee, we see all these fish out here, but I never really thought about the fact that some of them must eat others. . . . That damselfish was so busy chasing blue tangs away I'll bet it never even saw the skinny trumpetfish. I wonder why the damselfish chase all the other fish away, anyway?"

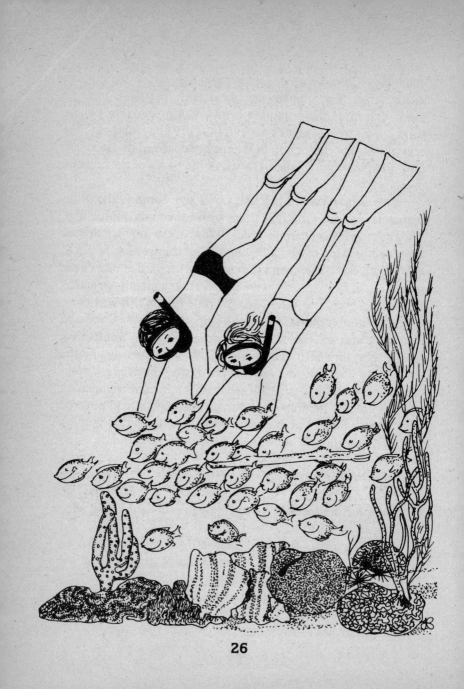

"Maybe if we watch them we'll be able to figure it out."

Coral and Tommy put their heads back into the water, breathing through their snorkels, and watched the damselfish. What fierce little fish they were! Each fish seemed to protect one area, and although the damselfish were only a couple of inches long—shorter than an average finger—they bravely chased away much bigger fish: trumpetfish (when they saw

them), parrotfish, blue-and-yellow queen angelfish, even other damselfish. To be able to watch the damselfish more closely, Coral and Tommy moved into shallower water—and if they got too close to the bottom, the damselfish nipped at them, too! But as soon as they backed away, the little fish returned to their territories, apparently satisfied that the threat was gone.

The children watched until their parents returned for lunch, and understood only that the damselfish seemed to be protecting their home areas. But why?

Their parents didn't know, either, so after lunch they asked Oliver: why did damselfish chase all the other fish away from what seemed to be dead coral?

Oliver bobbed up and down in his doorway, and answered their question with one of his own: "What do damselfish eat?"

"Other fish?" Coral guessed, thinking of the trumpetfish's hunt.

"Coral?" Tommy wondered, remembering the parrotfish.

"Wrong, and wrong again!" Oliver exclaimed. "Those damselfish eat algae, one of the few plants that can grow in the sea. But they don't like to travel around too far, like the blue tangs do, so they keep a sort of garden. All that dead coral the damselfish protect has algae growing on it; the damselfish want the algae for themselves, so they chase other fish—and even people—away from it." Oliver bobbed, pleased that he could explain these things. "They used to chase me away, too, so now I try to avoid them," he added. "Those little nips hurt!"

"How did you learn that, Oliver?" Coral asked. "We watched and watched, but we couldn't figure it out."

"You've only been here a few days, Coral," Oliver said kindly. "I've had a lot more time than that to watch the damsels. Did you two figure out what the trumpetfish was doing?"

"We saw it eat a damselfish!" Tommy said, still amazed. "It just hung around with the blue tangs, and when a damselfish was trying to get all those tangs away from its garden, the trumpetfish snuck up and sucked down the damsel!''

"So we figured the trumpetfish was trying to hide: in the soft coral, and along with the parrotfish, and then with the blue tangs. That way the little fish that it eats don't see it, and it has a chance to get them," Coral added.

"We never would have figured it out, either, if we hadn't actually seen the trumpetfish eat the damselfish—because even though the trumpetfish is long it's so skinny—its whole jaw stretched out when the damsel was inside! Wow!''

"For a mere fish, with no arms and no suckers, the trumpetfish manages to eat pretty well, I'd say," Oliver agreed. "I'm really impressed with what you've seen and learned. So many people come down here for days and days, scuba divers too, and they never stop swimming long enough to watch what's happening among the fishes! You know, there are lots of other fish that hide, too: lizardfish and scorpionfish and frogfish and—''

"Fish that look like lizards and scorpions and frogs? Really?'' Coral interrupted.

"Do trumpetfish look like trumpets?'' Oliver responded, annoyed.

"Oh! I'm sorry, Oliver, It's just that the names are so familiar, but the animals that have them seem so unusual! I guess a trumpetfish looks a *little* like a trumpet—especially when it opens its mouth so wide!''

"That's it, Coral. Whoever decided what names those fish should have must have named them because, in some way, the fish reminded them of the land animals. A lizardfish *does* have a mouth that's a little like a lizard's mouth. Scorpionfish don't look like scorpions, but they do have a venom—a poison that they can inject like a scorpion does. And frogfish . . . they gulp down their prey like a frog, I guess. Have you ever seen any of these fish?''

"No, not even in books.''

"My folks have talked about scorpionfish," Tommy remembered. "I think they even have a picture of one. It looks like a rock."

"That's the scorpionfish! Sometimes when I'm out hunting I walk right over one without even realizing it's there."

"Oliver, do you think that Tommy and I could see some of these hiding fish, even though we're only snorkeling?" Coral asked.

"If you can see a trumpetfish eat a damselfish, you can see anything! Stop by on your way in and tell me what you've found."

"Okay! See you later!"

4   Hidden Fish

Once they left Oliver, though, Coral wasn't sure where to start to look for fish that hid. Tommy thought the rocks near the dock might be a good place to begin, since scorpionfish looked like rocks.

And he was right. They hovered at the surface near the rocks for a few minutes, and Tommy shouted through his snorkel, "I think that rock is a scorpionfish! See the eyes?"

Coral looked and looked, but couldn't see a rock with eyes. Tommy pointed. Still she couldn't see it. He swam a little closer and pointed again. Suddenly one of the rocks swam away! *Now* she could see it! When the scorpionfish swam, it spread out its pectoral fins—the ones like arms—and they were shaped like fans, with beautiful red-and-brown patterns on them. When the scorpionfish stopped, it folded its pectoral fins in and the patterns disappeared again. So, for that matter, did the scorpionfish. At least it *seemed* to disappear. No wonder Coral hadn't been able to see it! When Oliver talked about fish that hid, he wasn't kidding! But now that she knew what to look for, Coral could see the eyes of the scorpionfish, looking like deep, dark holes in an algae-covered rock.

The snorkelers swam closer to the scorpionfish. This time it reacted by raising its dorsal fin, the fin on the top of its body. When they backed off, the fish lowered its fin and looked like a rock again.

"You know, Tommy," Coral commented, "it's as if the scorpionfish doesn't always want to hide. When it knows that we see it, it raises that fin, which makes it even more obvious. And when it swims we can easily see its pectoral fins. It's like playing Hide and Seek: when the person who's 'It' sees you, and you *know* they see you, it's no good trying to hide any more. You just run for base!"

"But the scorpionfish doesn't go far when it swims away," Tommy objected.

"Maybe that's because it knows it's poisonous. Once it's been seen, it just displays the fins that have the venom. As long as the people—or fish—who see it know about the venom, they'll leave it alone—sort of like a dog growling and baring its teeth!"

"That makes sense," Tommy agreed, "and even after the scorpionfish moves, once it puts its fins down, it blends into the background again like it's doing now, even though it's on a sandy bottom instead of the rocks. Hey! Look at those fish just on the edge of the sand! Don't their mouths remind you of—"

"A lizard!" Coral completed the sentence. "Just like Oliver said! But I only see *one* fish over there."

The lizardfish was sitting on top of the sand. Its body was long and thin, though not as thin as the trumpetfish's body. It was resting, leaning on its ventral, or bottom, fins. Its pectoral fins stuck straight out, like little wings on an airplane. Behind its wide, upside-down-'V'-shaped mouth, Coral could see its gills waving slowly.

"And it's not really hidden, either," Coral continued, disappointed.

"No, the one you're looking at isn't very hidden, Corrie. You're right about that. But there's another one!" Tommy was triumphant. "Look at the mark in the sand next to your lizardfish."

Coral looked. Sure enough, next to the lizardfish was a dark line in the sand. She looked more carefully, and could just make out the shape of the wide mouth of another lizardfish, almost completely buried in the sand.

"I see it now, Tommy. You're right—*that's* hidden! You know, it's funny: we look at a patch of sand, and it seems more empty than anywhere around. A glance over it shows hardly anything. But when we look more closely . . . there are all sorts of things hiding there! Do you see those two bumps?" She pointed. "I wonder if they're snails walking on the sand. But they're not crawling around or anything; they just seem to be swivelling. . . ."

They swam closer to the two bumps.

"Why, they look like *eyes!*" Coral exclaimed.

Tommy left the surface and swam down toward the two eyes. A fin raised up behind them, and the frilly edge of a *very* flat fish began to wriggle a little. Tommy surfaced and blew the water out of his snorkel.

"It's a flounder, I bet!"

33

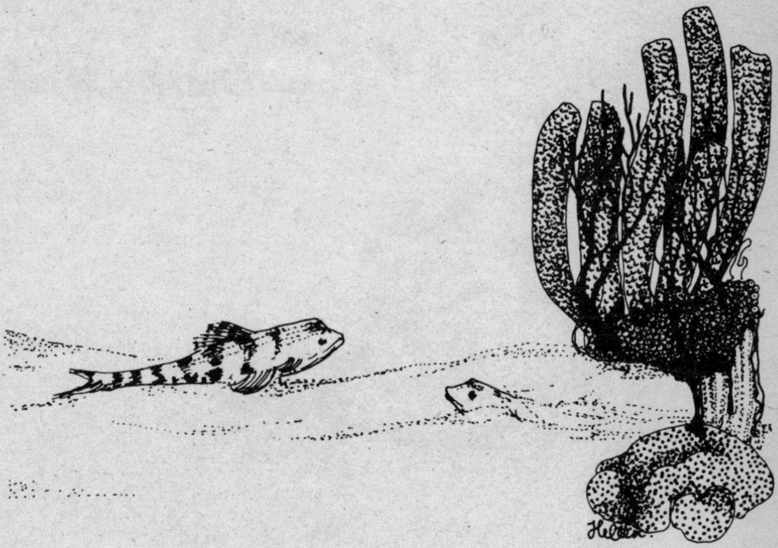

They continued to watch the fish. It shook the sand off its body, swam a few feet, and settled down on the rocks. As they watched the flounder, its body changed color from almost white like the sand, to a dark greenish-blue mottling. In a few seconds it seemed to disappear against the rocks, blending in perfectly with their colors. No wonder Coral and Tommy had had trouble seeing it!

"Tommy, I wonder why fish hide?"

"I guess so other fish, like trumpetfish, can't find them to eat them."

"But all fish don't hide—and all fish might be eaten by something else, wouldn't you think? The damselfish weren't hiding, and angelfish and parrotfish don't hide. . . . Maybe some fish hide so the fish *they* eat won't see them?"

"That makes sense, Corrie. If a damselfish thought the stuff on the back of a scorpionfish was part of his garden, and came around to take a nibble, it'd be easy for the scorpionfish to eat it! Imagine a bunch of blue tangs mobbing a scorpionfish to try to eat the algae on its skin! The scorpionfish could eat all it wanted—if the tangs weren't too big for it. Hey! Let's get some fish and see if we can feed a scorpionfish. Since it stays in one place, we could hold the fish close to its mouth and see what happens!"

"I like that idea, Tommy—but for tomorrow! Right now I'm chilly, and I can see the dive boats coming back, and I want to ask Oliver more about frogfish."

"And tell him that we found a hidden fish he hadn't told us about: the flounder! Let's go!" In a splash of fins, Tommy turned around and headed at full speed to Oliver's house. Coral followed, swimming as fast as she could; the fast swimming helped her to warm up.

5　Oliver the Magician

"Oliver, we found a scorpionfish and *two* lizardfish, and even a flounder!" Tommy cried.

"We're trying to figure out why the fish hide, and what they eat, and—" Coral exclaimed at the same time.

"Wait, wait, one at a time, please!" Oliver ordered, but he seemed pleased by their enthusiasm. "You found a scorpionfish and *two* lizardfish?"

"Yes, yes, and even a flounder!" Tommy affirmed. "When we first saw the flounder, it was almost buried in the sand, and almost completely white; Corrie only noticed it because of the way its eyes stuck out. Then it moved over to some rocks, and turned greenish—just like the rocks! How can it do that?"

"Oh, I know a little about changing colors," Oliver declared, modestly. He moved farther out of his house, and turned from gray, to reddish, to pale brown with dark spots. Then he changed the look of his skin, from smooth to bumpy. To make sure that the children had seen all of the changes, he displayed them again, slowly, and ended up his usual grayish-brown color.

"How did you *do* that, Oliver?" Tommy asked. "That was neat!"

Watching Oliver change colors reminded Coral of the first day she had seen him, when he had changed colors after Linda had touched him. At that time she'd been so excited about just seeing an octopus that she hadn't really thought about the color change. But now . . . *how* did *he do that?* she wondered.

"It's hard to explain, Tommy," Oliver answered. He bobbed up and down for a minute, then continued, "It sort of happens when I want it to, or when I'm worried, or excited, or frightened. Watch this."

Oliver left his house and climbed on top of the ledge above it. He flattened his body, sinking his eyes way down, and closed them to tiny slits. His skin became bumpy and took on the same brown, mottled coloration as the ledge. If Coral and Tommy hadn't known he was there they would never have noticed him. Then he scooted back into his doorway.

"It's a very handy skill to have, being able to camouflage myself like that," Oliver declared. "Once in a while when I'm hunting I see a moray eel out hunting too. Moray eels are okay—when they're not hungry, that is—but sometimes they like to eat octopuses! So I flatten out and stay very still, and most of the time they pass right by me."

"Oh Oliver, only most of the time? What happens the other times?" Coral asked.

"Well, when they *do* discover me, I just back up and hold out my suckers, like this." He demonstrated, rolling his arms up around his head so that all the children could see was lots of suckers. "The morays can't bite through the tough skin of my suckers, and while they're trying, I have a chance to grab them, or even to bite *them!* And if that doesn't work I just swim away, like this."

The octopus brought down his arms, and headfirst, with his arms trailing behind him, he zoomed through the water, swimming circles around Coral and Tommy.

"It's jet propulsion—I suck in the water and blow it out again, hard, and it pushes me along! An octopus," he bragged, bobbing of course, "can take care of himself. Um, as long as he sees his enemy before the enemy sees him. If we're taken by surprise, things can be a bit trickier."

"Then what happens?" Tommy asked.

"Then I don't disappear. Well, I *do* disappear, but whoever's chasing me doesn't know it until it's too late! Do you know what I mean?"

"Not at all!"

"Watch!" Oliver turned very dark. Then he seemed to be dissolving in the water! Another Oliver swam up to his doorway and entered. "Did you figure it out?" the "other" Oliver asked.

"It's your *ink!*" Coral exclaimed.

"You turned dark, then pumped out some ink that was in the same shape you were. While we were looking at that, you . . . what did you do then?" Tommy stopped, confused.

"I turned light again and swam away very fast!"

"It's just like the magicians do!" Tommy was delighted. "You got us looking at one thing and did something else while we weren't paying attention!"

"That's it!" Oliver said, lowering his eyes modestly, but

41

still bobbing up and down just a bit. "Who do you think the magicians learned that from in the first place?"

"And being able to camouflage yourself, and swim fast, and squirt ink, and protect yourself with your suckers, are all ways that you avoid animals that are trying to eat you—right, Oliver? Because none of those things will help you to find or catch shells to eat." Coral was thinking of Oliver's reasons for hiding, and comparing them with the reasons that scorpionfish, lizardfish, and flounders hid.

"Right!"

"But the other hiding fish we saw—I don't think they hide just to get away from hunters. . . . We thought they were hiding *because* they were hunters, so their prey wouldn't be able to see them!"

"We decided *that* after seeing so many other fish, like parrotfish, that don't hide at all," Tommy added.

"You two really *are* learning a lot. Maybe you can help *me* learn something: usually your lips are red, but now they're purple. Why is that?''

"Oh, because I'm co-o-old!" Coral exclaimed. "We've been in the water a long time today! Don't you get cold, Oliver?''

"No. My body temperature varies with the water around me. The same thing happens with fish. Otherwise, we'd be in trouble! People stay about the same temperature all the time, though, except when they're sick or very cold—like you are now. Maybe you should go get warm; I wouldn't want you to get sick and not be able to visit me!''

"Good idea! G'bye, Oliver!''

"Bye, Oliver! See you tomorrow!''

Coral and Tommy swam off, heading for nice warm sweatshirts and jeans. Even the Caribbean can be cold after a long time in the water.

GOTOMEER.

6 Tidepooling

At dinner that night Coral's father asked if the children would like to see a bit of the island the next day. "We thought we'd rent a car and look for flamingos, and see some other sights of Bonaire," he said. It sounded like fun, and since everyone wanted to be in the water at least part of the day, they would only be gone until lunchtime. Coral didn't want Oliver to miss them, and Tommy was still challenged by the thought of finding a frogfish.

It *was* fun, too. They drove along a lake and saw bright pink flamingos wading in the shallow water. They visited Lac Bay, a large enclosed bay that opened into the rough water on the windy side of Bonaire. There was a tiny beach at Lac, too, where Coral and Tommy met some island children, Chellie and Jimmy. Chellie could speak Papiamentu, the language of Bonaire, as well as some English and Dutch. Jimmy spoke Dutch but very little English, and Tommy and Coral could speak only English. But they all liked to swim, and managed to become friends even though they didn't always understand what the others were saying.

There was a huge pile of shells near the beach at Lac, and the children went over to look at it. "Why are all these shells here?" Tommy asked.

Chellie explained that the animal that made the shells, the queen conch, was very good to eat. People snorkeled for the conchs, removed the animals, and then left the shells in the pile on the beach. Anyone who wanted to take shells was welcome to.

The shells had been there a long time and were bleached by the sun. They weren't nearly as pretty as the shells Oliver had given Coral and Tommy, but they WERE a lot bigger. Oliver! "Tommy! Let's take one of these nice big shells to Oliver!"

Tommy agreed, "It'll make a nice decoration for his doorway, and it's big enough to protect him some, too."

"Oliver? Who's Oliver?" their new friends wanted to know.

"He's a friend of ours who lives in the sea," Tommy answered mysteriously. "Would you like to meet him?"

"Yes! When?"

"This afternoon?"

"Our uncle is coming over from Curaçao later, and we want to see him—but he leaves again tonight. Could we see Oliver tomorrow instead?" Chellie asked.

"Sure! We visit him every day."

"Maybe you could come to our house for lunch today—Jimmy and I could show you some animals along the edge of the sea there."

"But how will we get back to the hotel?" Coral asked. If Chellie and Jimmy lived too far away, she and Tommy wouldn't have any chance at all to see Oliver for the whole day!

"You can walk over to the hotel from our house," Chellie assured her. "It's not far at all."

So Coral's and Tommy's parents drove back to the hotel, and Coral and Tommy rode home with Chellie and Jimmy and their parents. After lunch the children walked along the sea shore. Instead of a sandy beach, there was a rocky shoreline with puddles of seawater that filled every day at high tide. Now the tide was low, and the children could wade through the tidepools.

The first thing they saw was a little flat crab, but before anyone had time to point at it, it had scurried under a rock. Jimmy lifted up the edge of the rock, and the crab scurried even farther underneath it. What a funny little crab! It didn't matter what language they spoke—that crab made everyone laugh.

On the underside of Jimmy's rock were a lot of small shells, tightly attached to the rock. Tommy pulled one off, and inside it they saw two small bumps. The shell was mostly white, but around the bumps it was scarlet. "Tooth shell," Chellie explained, pointing to one of her teeth. The bumps *did* look like teeth—and bleeding ones, at that!

Coral tried lifting a rock. In a flash of movement and color an eel zipped out and swam between her feet, over the edge of the tidepool, and into deeper water. It happened so fast Coral didn't even have time to worry about her toes! Not that the eel seemed very scary; it was more frightened than Coral had been.

Tommy lifted another rock and found a black lump on its underside. "Put the rock back in the water, upside down," Chellie directed. As they watched, the black lump acquired an oval shape, like a slug. Slowly, tiny frilled arms emerged from its back.

"Can it hurt us?" Coral asked.

Jimmy shook his head "no," so Tommy picked the thing up and held it in his hand beneath the surface of the water. The an-

imal crawled along on Tommy's hand like a snail, and it turned out to be something very like a snail—but without a shell. It was a nudibranch. "Nudibranch" means "naked gills," and the frilly "arms" were its gills, the way it breathed in the water. A fish's gills are inside its body, but those of a nudibranch are outside, or naked. This name made more sense to the children than "lizardfish," once they understood it!

Each child held the nudibranch in his hand and felt it crawl along; then Tommy put the animal back on its rock and turned the rock over the same way he had found it.

Near that rock Coral spotted a pale green creature with brown spots, a sea hare. It had more shape than the nudibranch, but not much more. One end of it looked a little like a rabbit's head, with tiny perky "ears." Coral touched it gently. It *felt* like the nudibranch, too, very smooth but not slimy at all. Chellie had never touched one of those animals, so she also

bent down to stroke it—but she lost her balance and hit it harder than she'd intended. Dark red color began to spread through the water!

"Oh, Chellie, did you cut yourself?"

Chellie shook her head.

"Then—could it be that the sea hare is bleeding? It doesn't look hurt, though." The sea hare had crawled through the cloud of red and didn't seem to be injured at all.

"I've got it! The sea hare inked, just like Ol—an octopus, that is—does!" Suddenly it made sense to Tommy; he was so excited that he'd nearly given away the secret of Oliver! "It got scared when Chellie accidentally hit it, so it inked!"

"I'll bet you're right, Tommy! And I want to ask Oliver about it right away!" Coral realized that if they didn't get back soon, they might not get to see Oliver today.

"We'll see you tomorrow morning, right?" Coral asked Chellie and Jimmy.

51

"Sure!" Jimmy said. "Bye!"

"Goodbye!" Chellie said.

Waving, Coral and Tommy climbed up to the road and began the short walk back to the hotel. Behind them, Chellie and Jimmy jumped into the water for a swim.

7   A Fish Goes Fishing

Back at the hotel, Coral and Tommy found the shell from Lac Bay, grabbed their snorkeling gear, managed to persuade the cook to give them a piece of fish, and headed for Oliver's house.

"I missed you this morning!" Oliver told them.

"Our folks drove us around the island today," Tommy said. "They didn't tell us we were going until last night, so we had no chance to tell you."

"We missed you, too, Oliver," Coral said, "and when we saw the conch shells at Lac Bay, we thought of you. Those shells aren't as pretty as the ones you have at your doorway, but they're bigger, and prettier than a tin can! So we brought you the best one we could find. Hope you like it!"

"It's lovely!" Oliver exclaimed. "It will fit perfectly right here." And he put their conch shell just next to his doorway in front of all the other decorations. "What are you going to do this afternoon?"

"We don't have much time left, I guess. . . . We've got a piece of fish we thought you might like, and we wanted to try to offer some to a scorpionfish—if we could find a scorpionfish. And we're still trying to find a frogfish!"

"Ah, a frogfish. *That's* one of the reasons I was missing you this morning: a frogfish showed up last night and settled on the rocks near where you saw the scorpionfish yesterday. Maybe

with your sharp eyes you'll be able to spot him. As for the fish,'' Oliver continued, ''don't mind if I do have a morsel. It *is* a nice change of pace.''

Tommy tore the piece of fish in half and held one piece out to Oliver. Bobbing, the octopus gently took the gift and placed it beneath his body. ''A nice snack for me to nibble on while you two go frogfish hunting.''

''Um . . . what do frogfish look like?'' Coral asked.

''Oh, that's right! We never did talk about that!'' Oliver bobbed vigorously. ''A frogfish looks like a sponge more than anything else. It's kind of lumpy, and shaped a little like a scorpionfish. But its eyes are smaller, and since it doesn't have any venom it has to hide better than a scorpionfish does. I don't want to tell you any more; I'll let you be surprised. Be sure to stop by and tell me what you saw!''

''Sure thing, Oliver!'' Tommy said, and thought, *Interesting . . . saying ''Oliver'' through my snorkel doesn't sound nearly as silly today as I thought it did yesterday.*

They went off to the rocky ledge. Coral was determined to find the scorpionfish—or the frogfish—or both—on her own today. She looked and looked. She and Tommy swam slowly back and forth along the ledge, until at last Coral saw something that didn't quite fit in. It was a rock, sort of, but its shape was more fishlike, and somehow it looked soft. She swam closer and noticed it was moving very slightly. It *was* a fish—it must be the frogfish!

"Tommy! Tommy! Here's the frogfish!" she shouted.

Tommy, searching farther down the ledge, didn't hear her, so Coral swam over to him. "I've found the frogfish!" she announced proudly.

"Where?"

"It's right over here . . . let me see . . . ." Where *was* the frogfish? It was just there; she didn't think it had moved in such a short time, but it blended in so well . . . . Ah! "There it is!"

"Where? Oh, *there!* Wow, what a fish!"

The frogfish *did* look more like a sponge than anything else. Its tiny eyes looked like the little holes in a sponge. It was a brownish-sandy color with some darker brown spots, like a silt-covered sponge. The frogfish didn't have gill flaps like most fish—even the well-hidden scorpionfish had large gill flaps which waved in and out noticeably when it breathed. The scorpionfish had rested on its fins, but the fins had still looked like regular fish fins. On the frogfish, those fins looked just like arms, with elbows and everything! And just where the "arms" met the fish's body—*its armpits*, Tommy thought—were short tubes that waved as water flowed through them.

"Those must be its gills, over there in its armpits," he reasoned. "They sure don't look like the gills of a regular fish. How *weird!*"

"What *is* that on its head?" Coral was looking at a short, funny-looking wormy thing in between the frogfish's eyes, just in front of its dorsal fin. "Everything else looks like part of a sponge except that."

"Maybe it's not part of the fish. Maybe it's just some kind of worm crawling along on the frogfish, thinking it's a sponge? Hey! I still have part of that fish we got from the kitchen. Do you think the frogfish would eat it?"

"It might. If we're right about hidden fish being fish-eaters, it ought to be happy with a free meal."

Coral and Tommy were in very shallow water, and the fish there were used to being fed by snorkelers. Before Tommy could get the piece of fish close to the frogfish, lots of other little fish were nibbling at it. Tommy tried to wave the little fish away, but they just came right back. Finally, little fish and all, he held the piece of food right in front of the frogfish's mouth.

What happened next happened so fast that if both of them hadn't seen it they would never have believed it. The little wormy thing left the frogfish's forehead and extended out in front of its mouth, and Coral and Tommy could see that it was attached to the frogfish by what looked exactly like a short piece of fishing line. The frogfish had a fishing lure!

As Tommy held the bait, the lure attracted some of the little fish that were mobbing the bait—and in a flash, the frogfish leaped forward and gulped down one of the little fish! The frogfish didn't "aim," like the trumpetfish had by waving its head back and forth; the frogfish gave no warning at all. One second there were a whole bunch of little fish attacking the bait, and the next second there were a whole bunch of little fish minus one!

Coral was so amazed that her mouth fell open away from her snorkel and she swallowed a mouthful of water! Coughing, she stood up in the shallow water to catch her breath.

Tommy stood up too. "Am I crazy, or did I really just see what I thought I saw? A *fish* going fishing?"

"Yes, yes!" Coral gasped. "If you're crazy, then so am I! Let's go tell Oliver!"

"Wait—we haven't tried to feed a scorpionfish yet, and there's still some food left. Maybe we can find the one we saw yesterday. It was right around here. . . ." Tommy swam off, looking.

Coral cleared the water from her snorkel and put her face back into the water to watch the frogfish again. It looked exactly as it had when she'd first found it, sitting quietly and innocently on the rocks. There was one difference: its stomach was a lot bigger!

She joined Tommy just as he found the scorpionfish. He swam down and held the bait near its mouth, but nothing happened. Soon he had to return to the surface to breathe. "The little fish don't mob the bait here because it's deeper, I guess. But I can't hold the food very still or for very long. Do you want to try, Corrie?"

Coral took the bait and swam down with it to the scorpionfish. When she held the piece of fish near its mouth it seemed to be interested, but before anything else could happen she needed to go up for air. Since no other fish were trying to eat the bait, she left it on the bottom in front of the scorpionfish. She swam up to the surface, cleared her snorkel, and looked back down at the scorpionfish. The bait was gone!

"He ate the bait!" Tommy shouted. "While you were swimming up, he flared out his pectoral fins for a second and just sucked down that piece of fish." They kept on watching the scorpionfish; it opened its mouth wide in a quick motion, and a few scraps of fish came out. "I think he just burped." Tommy giggled. "We've got to tell Oliver about this!"

Coral led the way to their friend's home, and they told him what they had seen.

"I forgot to tell you the other name for frogfish, I guess," Oliver said, but something about the way he said it made them suspect he'd done it on purpose. "They're also called 'angler-fish.' "

"Anglerfish," Coral repeated. "And fishermen are called 'anglers'. . . so frogfish *are* fish that go fishing, just like Tommy said! That was the most amazing thing I've ever seen."

"More amazing than the trumpetfish hunting? More amazing than *I* am when I change colors and disappear?" Oliver demanded.

"Nothing could be more amazing than *you,* Oliver!" Coral corrected herself. "You're not even in the same category as all those other things! You're a friend with special talents."

Oliver was pleased. He bobbed up and down. "What's next on your schedule?"

"A race back to the dock! It's almost dinnertime!" Tommy said. "Bye, Oliver!"

"Bye, Oliver! We'll see you tomorrow. Oh, and we'd like to introduce you to two new friends of ours, if you don't mind."

"It would be a privilege," Oliver bobbed.

Tommy won the race. But then, he'd had a head start.

8 The Disappearance

The next day, as Coral and Tommy were finishing breakfast, Chellie and Jimmy arrived at the hotel.

"You're early," Tommy said. "Would you like some mango or toast?"

"No thanks, we've already had breakfast. We're excited about meeting your mystery friend Oliver," Chellie told him, and Jimmy nodded in agreement. Coral and Tommy had their snorkeling gear with them, so they wished their parents a good dive, said goodbye, and headed for the dock.

They got their gear on, jumped in, and began swimming to Oliver's house. Coral was in the lead; she'd missed spending much time with Oliver yesterday and was excited about introducing him to their new friends. Soon she could see Oliver's doorway with its decorations of shells and a tin can. She was too excited to notice that the conch shell from Lac Bay wasn't there.

But as soon as Coral arrived, she realized that something was wrong. Instead of Oliver waiting at his doorway, she could only see the black prickly spines of a long-spined sea urchin!

"Oliver's not here!"

Tommy looked around. "He must be! Maybe he's behind that urchin." He dove down for a closer look and came up shaking his head. They all stood up in the shallow water. "There's nothing back there."

"Where could he be?" Coral cried, worried. "Yesterday when I told him we were going to bring Chellie and Jimmy to meet him he seemed so pleased! I—I'm afraid something's happened to him!"

Chellie and Jimmy looked bewildered. Coral explained that their friend was an octopus. "But not just any octopus," she continued, "Oliver talked to us! And he helped us to learn so much about all the animals in the sea, and he said he'd be here today!"

"And he showed us how he could hide, and swim, and squirt ink," Tommy added. "And now he's gone!"

Jimmy had figured out from the shells at the den that Oliver was an octopus, but he still didn't understand why Coral and Tommy were so upset. Chellie explained to him in Dutch, and Jimmy answered her, sounding confident.

"Jimmy says that octopuses move their houses a lot," she translated. "Maybe some animal discovered Oliver's house and Oliver thought it'd be safer to leave. Jimmy thinks we'll probably find Oliver's new house close to his old one. Jimmy knows a lot about the animals; he snorkels in front of our house every day," she concluded proudly.

"But what if the animal that discovered Oliver's house—" Coral couldn't finish. The thought was too awful to put into words.

"No, Corrie, remember that Oliver showed us how an octopus can take care of itself."

"Sure," Chellie agreed. "I'll bet the four of us can find Oliver's new house really fast!"

That idea made more sense than any other, and doing something was a lot better than just worrying. The children began to search along the ledge, slowly. At every promising spot one of them would dive down for a closer look. Suddenly Jimmy shouted, "Octopus!"

And under the ledge they could all see the arms and suckers of an octopus! Coral called, "Oliver! It's us!" and extended her hand to the octopus. It moved farther back under the ledge.

Tommy dived down. "Oliver? Is that you?" The octopus shrank back still farther until it was out of sight.

Tommy sighed. "It's an octopus, all right. But it isn't Oliver."

They kept on searching. While he was looking, Tommy realized that some small spongy things he'd noticed before weren't sponges at all, but nudibranchs. When he picked one up he could see its snail-like underside. It was white, and instead of having an arm-like gill cluster, like the black one they had found yesterday, it had ruffled gills all along its back. They were patterned with blue and green and pink lines, and were very pretty. But they weren't Oliver, and the discovery wasn't nearly as much fun without Oliver to tell about it.

Jimmy found a sea urchin under the ledge. It didn't have long nasty-looking spines like the one in Oliver's house; its spines were short and white. A bunch of pebbles and some shells were stuck to the top of the urchin. "Watch!" Jimmy commanded, and he placed the urchin on his hand, under the water. Then he turned his hand upside-down. The urchin stayed attached to his hand, and the pebbles stayed attached to the urchin!

Jimmy gently rocked the urchin off his hand and gave it to Coral. *How did it stick to Jimmy?* she wondered, examining it through the smooth surface of the water. She saw what looked like little hairs between the urchin's spines, some stuck to the pebbles and shells, some waving free. The little hairs were tube feet, Coral realized. The suction of the tube feet held the pebbles and shells on the urchin so it could hide itself; the tube feet on the underside of the urchin would hold it in place on the sea bottom. Coral placed the urchin on her hand and felt the tightening sensation as the tube feet attached to her. When she turned her hand over, the urchin stayed right in place!

"Hey, that's neat! Can I try?" asked Tommy. He took the urchin carefully from Coral and placed it on his own hand, and they all watched it stick when he turned his hand over. Then he gave the urchin back to Jimmy.

"Look!" Jimmy said, pointing between the spines of the urchin.

"Why, the spines are moving! I didn't know the spines could move from one spot on the urchin to another!" Coral exclaimed.

Chellie giggled. "The spines aren't moving, Corrie; you

were right that they can't move that way. Jimmy's pointing to a little shrimp!''

Coral looked more closely and poked gently at the shrimp with her little finger. It jumped to the top of the spines and then backed down between them again away from her finger.

"I get it now! The shrimp's body is black like the urchin's body, and its claws are white. When it backs down between the spines and holds its claws up, it looks just like two more spines. You can't even see its body!''

Seeing the shrimp hide so well only reminded Coral of how well Oliver could hide.

They searched all morning. They looked along the ledge, and under the dock, and around the sand. They looked in crevices in coral heads and inside sponges and beneath the dive boat moorings. They found scorpionfish and anemones and a pair of banded coral shrimp—but no Oliver.

They searched until they were cold, then swam fast for a while to warm up and searched some more. They searched until the dive boats came in, and they kept on searching until they had to leave the water for lunch. No Oliver.

Chellie and Jimmy stayed for lunch, but it wasn't a very happy meal.

"We have to go now," Chellie told them after lunch.

"Oh, Chellie, I'm afraid we haven't shown you a very good time," Coral said. "We promised to introduce you to Oliver, and he wasn't there, and then we kept you in the water all morning trying to find him."

"It's okay. We understand, really. We just hope you find your friend."

"Thanks for helping us," Tommy said. "We'll let you know what happens."

"Yes, thanks again for helping us," Coral agreed. "And thanks for believing us, too!"

"Of *course* we believe you! I just hope we get to meet Oliver," Chellie said. "Bye!"

"Bye!" said Jimmy, and they left for home.

After saying goodbye to Chellie and Jimmy, Coral and Tommy returned to their parents' table.

"You two don't seem very happy today," Coral's mother remarked.

"We can't find our octopus; we miss him," Coral replied. Their parents knew about the octopus; they just didn't know that he talked.

"We have an idea that might take your minds off that problem," Tommy's mother said.

"Yes, we've been really impressed with how much you've been enjoying the water, and how much you've been learning," Coral's mother added. "Corrie, we're so glad you're enjoying the sea!"

"How would you like to learn to scuba dive?" Tommy's father asked them. "We've discussed it with Linda, and she thinks you'd make great divers. Usually she doesn't take students who are so young, but she's as impressed with you as we are."

Scuba lessons! Coral and Tommy both had the same thought: if they could scuba dive, they could explore deeper places than they could by snorkeling—so maybe while scuba diving they could find Oliver!

Their sad expressions brightened. "We'd love it!" they said together. "When do we start?"

"How about this afternoon? Be sure to do everything Linda says!"

Coral and Tommy didn't hear anything after "this afternoon." They were thinking about finding Oliver.

9 Scuba

Linda was waiting when Coral and Tommy arrived at the dive shop that afternoon. "I'm really glad you two will be learning to scuba dive," she told them. "Usually I don't like to teach people who are under fifteen years old, but you're pretty special. I've seen you snorkeling every day—and I'm glad I'll have the chance to show you some of my favorite parts of the reef! But you must remember: scuba diving *can* be dangerous. Just because you're comfortable in the water doesn't mean that everything you might want to do is safe. Remember that what I'm teaching you is not a full course, and that you'll only be learning enough to be safe when you're with me or another certified instructor."

Coral and Tommy listened carefully.

"I hope that after we've dived, you'll want to take a full scuba course back in the U.S. In a full course, the divers learn what they need to know to make their own decisions underwater. They don't have to dive with an instructor."

"Are we old enough for that?" Tommy asked.

"Yes, for what's called Junior Certification. That means you must dive with a certified diver, preferably one of your parents. Then, when you turn fifteen, you can get full certification.

"Scuba training can be a funny thing: some people take scuba courses just to keep a friend company, or to have something to do. They learn *how* to dive but not *why,* so they get bored underwater—''

''Divers get *bored?* On *Bonaire?''* Coral was amazed.

''Well, not too often on Bonaire,'' Linda admitted. ''Anyway, that's why it's important to me to understand why my students want to scuba dive. Corrie?''

To find Oliver, Coral thought, but she didn't say it out loud. Anyway, finding Oliver would be wonderful, but there were other reasons, too. ''Remember what you told me about watching the animals and trying to figure out why they do things?'' she asked Linda.

''Of course!''

''I guess that's why I want to be able to dive. Tommy and I have seen lots of terrific things snorkeling, but sometimes we're way up at the surface and the animals seem so far away. I'd like to be able to get closer to them so I can see them better.''

''Sounds like a pretty good reason to me. Tommy, why do *you* want to be able to scuba dive?''

''I think I'll be able to find things better if I can get closer to the bottom,'' Tommy replied, thinking about a very special octopus. ''We've found a lot of hidden fish, like a scorpionfish and a flounder. I'll bet if we were closer we could find a lot more!''

''You saw a scorpionfish? And a flounder, too? That's terrific! I should have known that such enthusiastic snorkelers would have good reasons to learn to dive. Now, let's sit down over here and I'll explain a few things before we get wet.'' Linda walked over to a table with a set of scuba gear on top of it. Their lessons had begun.

Linda told them that the word ''scuba'' meant Self Contained Underwater Breathing Apparatus, then showed them the equipment and explained the purpose of all the gear. ''Anyone can breathe underwater,'' she said. ''The trickiest part of scuba diving is something lots of people never think about: being able to float in mid-water, like an angelfish or a filefish does. Once you can hover like a helicopter, without kicking or waving your hands all over the place, *then* you can consider yourself a diver.''

At last they were ready to, as Linda called it, ''get wet''—in the pool, at first. They helped each other to gear up. ''You look funny, Tommy!'' Coral giggled. ''Are you ready to do a moon walk?''

''Hey, now, you're not joking as much as you think, Corrie,'' Linda said. ''Scuba divers, like astronauts, enter an alien world where there is no air for them to breathe. There's no gravity as we know it, either, which is one thing I've always liked about diving: when I trip, I don't fall down!''

Tommy jumped into the pool first, with Coral and Linda close behind him. They settled to the bottom and breathed. What a feeling—being underwater and breathing! It was noisier than Coral had expected; she could hear her bubbles every time she breathed out. Linda showed them that they could turn somersaults in mid-water, and after a few turns they got down to the business of training exercises. They learned how to clear any water out of their masks without having to go to the surface, and how to hover. Hovering was fun! After a little experimentation, both Coral and Tommy could sit in mid-water with their legs crossed as if they were sitting on a chair—but there was no chair, only water and scuba equipment.

Then they swam around the bottom of the pool with their masks off, and found they could see pretty well anyway, even without the masks. It was kind of nice to know that if their masks fell off, or somehow got kicked off, they could still see—and see well enough to find the mask, and know how to put it on and get the water out of it. Linda would be keeping track of how deep they went and where they went, but they were learning skills that would help them in an emergency.

Soon Linda signalled them to the shallow end of the pool, and everyone stood up. ''You guys picked up all the skills even

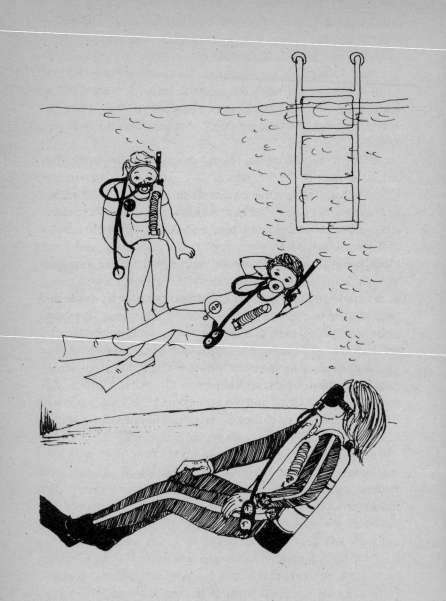

faster than I thought you would!'' she said. ''You're what I call 'instant divers.' ''

'' 'Instant divers?' '' they asked.

''Sure—just add water! Why don't you take a few minutes to swim around here and make sure you're really comfortable. Then we'll go for a short dive in the sea!''

Hearing the compliment—and the plan—got Coral and Tommy so excited that they turned a bunch of flips in the water. Pretty soon the pool began to seem awfully tame. They were ready for the real thing.

They took their fins off, climbed out of the pool, and walked down to the dock. The tanks were heavy, but they were easier to wear than to carry. Besides, being able to scuba dive in the ocean would be worth whatever trouble it took.

On the dock they leaned on each other and put their fins back on.

''Wouldn't it be nice to be able to just go into the water and swim around like a fish?'' Coral said. ''I don't mind the equipment 'cause it's the only way we can breathe underwater. But it'd be so nice if we could breathe underwater without it!''

''Imagine a fish with this kind of equipment, walking around on land.'' Tommy laughed. ''It's incredible how different the water world is from the land world!''

''Yup! So here we go, into Planet Ocean!''

10 The First Dive

They stayed in very shallow water for this first dive, and
Linda headed straight toward Oliver's house. *She doesn't know
he's gone,* Coral realized, and sure enough, Linda seemed surprised to find only an urchin there. She shrugged and swam on
to her favorite coral head, the one she had shown Coral on their
snorkeling trip together. With the scuba equipment, Coral and
Tommy could rest on the sand around the coral head and watch
the moray eel they'd only seen from the surface before. His
mouth opened and closed slowly, and when they looked at him
head-on, his expression seemed quite friendly.

Linda brought them up to the anemone and showed them the
little shrimp that lived inside. *She doesn't realize we've already met those shrimp,* Tommy thought. Then Linda took a
piece of hotdog from her wetsuit pocket and dropped it near the
anemone. One of the anemone's arms touched the hotdog and
suddenly pulled back, taking the hot dog along with it. *That's
what it did with Tommy's hand that day,* Coral thought.

One disadvantage of the scuba gear seemed to be that they
couldn't talk the way they could while they were snorkeling.
Then, clearly, they heard Linda say, ''WATCH THIS!'' She
held her hand near the anemone, and the little shrimp jumped
out and swarmed over her hand. ''CLEANER SHRIMP.''

We were right about those shrimp being cleaners, Coral
thought. Suddenly she realized that Linda had been *talking* to

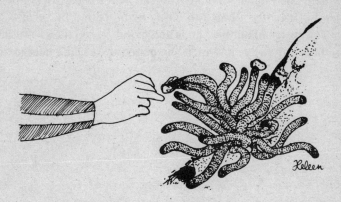

them, underwater, through her scuba mouthpiece! Scuba div-ing wasn't so different from snorkeling after all.

Linda pointed to her watch and signalled that it was time to head for shore. On the way in, they passed a scorpionfish. That is, *Linda* passed it. Tommy saw it and tugged on Linda's fin. When she turned around he pointed to the scorpionfish. "WATCH," they heard. Linda settled down to the bottom and slowly extended her hand to the scorpionfish. The fish raised its venomous dorsal spines. Linda held still until the spines were lowered, then moved her hand close again. This time the dorsal spines stayed down. She touched the scorpionfish on its side, below the dorsal spines, and began to stroke it gently. Then she moved her hand to its chin and stroked it there. Fi-nally, she moved her hand beneath its body and carefully lifted it up. The scorpionfish must have studied rocks long enough to know that rocks can't swim because it simply sat on Linda's hand as if she were part of the bottom!

"CAN I TRY?" Coral asked through her mouthpiece, and heard Linda say "SURE!" Linda pointed to the fish's dorsal fin and signalled "no," and Coral nodded her understanding. Then, very carefully, Linda placed the scorpionfish on Coral's outstretched hands. Tommy reached over and stroked the fish gently. It really seemed to enjoy being petted like that!

Tommy held out his hands and Coral placed the scorpionfish in them carefully, and then she petted it. It had a neat texture, too: it felt dry! A funny thought—she was underwater, and the fish was underwater, so how in the world could it feel *dry?*

Linda pointed to her watch again. Tommy slowly let the co-operative scorpionfish down in exactly the same place he had found it, and they swam back to the dock.

They rinsed and hung up the scuba equipment they'd been using and joined Linda at the table for their "debriefing."

"You were *super!*" Linda told them. "I'd be pleased to have you as my dive buddies anytime. What did you think about the way the scorpionfish felt?"

"Neat!" Tommy said.

"Surprising!" Coral added. "It felt dry, and I never expected a fish to feel dry underwater."

"So you noticed that, did you? That's one thing I like to do when I dive: find out how things feel. Scorpionfish feel dry, anemones feel sticky, and tomorrow I'll show you a critter that feels just like Velcro. It's fun to be able to do more than just look around underwater—I like to touch the sea, too. But you sure can't touch what you don't see! You have good eyes, Tommy; how'd you spot that scorpionfish? I must've swum right over it!"

"Well, we found one yesterday in nearly the same spot, so I was looking real hard in case it was still around," he explained.

"Of course—How could I forget how much snorkeling you two have been doing. You must have a pretty good idea of what that reef looks like, from the top, anyway. What other critters have you seen?"

"We told you about the flounder, right?"

"Right, Corrie."

"Did we tell you about the frogfish?"

"You found a *frogfish?* And you didn't tell me? Do you remember where it was?"

"Oh, yes!"

"Then we'll spend some time tomorrow on a frogfish hunt.

75

With any kind of luck, it'll still be around the same spot and I can come back later to photograph it. We hardly ever see frog-fish around here—they're a real treat. And I have a treat in mind for you at the end of our dive tomorrow, too.''

"What is it?''

"Ah, that's a surprise. You'll see tomorrow. Why don't you invite your parents to come along on the dive with us? Do you think they'd like that?''

"Oh, yes, Linda! Do *they* know about the surprise?'' Coral asked.

"I hope they do—my mom never can keep a secret from me!'' Tommy added.

"That's why they don't know, either. I'll see you in the morning. Be sure to get a good night's sleep.''

"We'll try! Bye, Linda!''

"Goodbye! See you in the morning!''

Coral was so concerned for Oliver, and excited about being able to search for him the next day, that she was afraid she wouldn't be able to sleep that night. But once she got into bed the long day—with Oliver's disappearance, and the search for him, and the scuba lesson, and the dive—all caught up with her. She fell asleep and dreamed of doing somersaults over the reef with Oliver Octopus.

11   Reunited

When Coral woke up it was barely light outside; the roosters had just begun to crow. She put on a bathing suit, slipped out of her room, and went down to the dock. Sitting there watching the sunlight over the sea, she thought what a wonderful thing the ocean was—and how impossible it was to describe. Not the books she'd read, not even the photographs she'd seen—nothing could create the feeling that she got while actually looking at the sea.

Now the sea held a secret: the location of one unique octopus named Oliver. He'd only been missing for one day, but it seemed like forever. *If I just knew he was okay,* Coral thought, *all that water out there would hold a wonderful secret. But since I don't know, it looks scary. . . ."*

Glumly, she turned onto her stomach and looked over the edge of the dock. In the shallow water she could see some long-spined urchins heading for cover. Little fish just up from their night's rest were swimming around in a groggy way. If they'd had hands, Coral felt sure they'd be rubbing their eyes! She began to feel a little better.

A movement way out in deep water caught her attention, and she sat up for a better look. It was dolphins! They were rolling along, a whole group of them, their shiny backs breaking the surface. They were close enough for her to see bursts of spray as they exhaled through their blowholes. Suddenly one

leaped from the water and dove in again, and soon they were all leaping gaily. In the early morning quiet Coral could hear the splashes they made when they entered the water. It was a beautiful sight, and suddenly the ocean didn't look at all frightening. Surely Oliver was okay.

Tommy came running onto the dock. "Here you are!" he said. "What're you looking—*wow!* Dolphins!"

They watched, fascinated, until the dolphins were out of sight. "I'll bet those dolphins bring us luck, Corrie," Tommy said. "Somehow I feel sure we're going to find Oliver today."

"Corrie and Tommy saw dolphins swimming by this morning!" Coral's mother told Linda when they all got to the dive shop. "Does that happen very often?"

"Have you ever dived with them, Linda?" Coral asked.

"They were jumping out of the water!" Tommy exclaimed.

"One at a time!" Linda laughed. "We see dolphins once in a while here; they just seem to be passing through, though, and never stay for very long. I wish they would. . . . And to answer your question, Corrie, whenever we get into the water with them they keep just out of sight. Once in a while a dolphin somewhere seems to befriend people, but it hasn't happened here . . . yet. Are you ready to dive?"

"Absolutely!" everyone chorused.

"Then let's get all this gear down to the dock."

Just before they entered the water, Linda said, "Okay, now, a few reminders. First of all, remember never to hold your breath. Second, be sure to equalize the pressure in your ears often. Third, I want Corrie and Tommy to stick close to me, and the rest of you folks can come along behind or beside us, okay?"

Everyone nodded.

"Since Corrie and Tommy were so good in the water yesterday, I'll be able to do more than just shepherd you all around on this dive; I'll get to show you some special things. Yesterday I introduced the kids to a Scotch tape animal—an anemone—and I promised 'em that today they'd touch a Velcro animal. It's a crinoid, and since it's related to starfish sometimes people call it a 'feather star'—you'll know why when you see one. And when you run your finger along one of the feathers, you'll know why I call them Velcro animals! Another one of their relatives is the sea urchin—would you like to hold one of those guys?''

"Yes!" Tommy said.

"Won't it hurt us?" his mother asked.

"Hey, I wouldn't do anything that would hurt you! This is a heart urchin, with very short spines, and if you look carefully you'll see a tiny hitchhiker living in between the spines. I know that Tommy and Coral will find it—if they can find a frogfish they can find anything! I hope they'll show us that frogfish on this dive, too.''

"For sure . . . if we can find it!"

"Ah, the pressure's on you kids now!" Corrie's mother laughed. "We've never seen a frogfish—think of it as your reward to us for bringing you to Bonaire!"

"They'll find it—I have total faith in them!" Linda said. "I'd also like to introduce everyone to a friend of mine, a spotted moray eel I call Mr. Greedy.''

"Is that the eel in your favorite coral head, Linda?" Coral asked. She'd seen the scared look on her mother's face when Linda mentioned the eel's name. "He has a cute face.''

"That's the eel, Corrie." Linda had seen the look, too. "When I first met him he was really . . . frisky; now I ought to change his name to Mr. Gregarious! But you'll soon be able to decide for yourselves." She held up a peanut can. "I'll be bringing some food along for Mr. Greedy and the fish, if you'd like to watch me feed them.''

"Great!" Tommy exclaimed. "I've fed fish before, but never an eel. Can we do it too?"

"Hey, Tom, you can't do *everything* on this dive—there'll

80

be others," Tommy's father cautioned. "Is there anything else, Linda?"

"That's about it. Oh, please let me know when you've used half the air in your tank by showing me your pressure gauge, and we'll begin moseying back to shore. After the surprise, of course!"

"What surprise?" Coral's father asked.

"Why, if I told you it wouldn't be a surprise, would it?" Linda told him with a twinkle in her eye.

"Hm-m-m . . ." he replied.

Linda jumped into the water, with Coral and Tommy close behind. Their parents soon joined them.

As usual, Linda went straight to her favorite coral head. She took a piece of fish from the peanut can and held it near Mr. Greedy. Everyone knelt in a circle and watched. At first the eel didn't seem to know the food was there; then suddenly he came out and grabbed it from Linda's hand. In a flash he swallowed the food. Linda fed the eel a few more pieces of fish, then held her hand flat on the sand, palm up. The eel moved forward to investigate her hand with little tubes above his mouth, his external nostrils. Linda began to stroke the eel gently beneath his mouth, and he seemed to enjoy it, rolling his head from side to side.

Waving goodbye to Mr. Greedy, Linda said "FROG-FISH?" Tommy and Coral led the way to the rocky spot and began to search. Soon Coral found the funny little fish and pointed to it. Linda took out her regulator mouthpiece, grinned broadly, and signalled OK—but the other adults looked confused. Tommy made a circle around the frogfish with his finger, but it looked so much like a sponge they still couldn't see it. Finally Linda touched it gently—just enough to cause it to move a bit—and then everyone could tell that the "sponge" was a frogfish. Coral's father pointed to the children, then signalled OK—to say YOU are OKAY!

And they replied with a smile and a shrug—Aw, it's nothing.

Smiling at the charade, Linda led them toward deeper water where the reef sloped off sharply. This was the first time Coral and Tommy had seen the dropoff, and it was wonderful! Ahead of them was only clear blue water; below them, the slope of corals. Linda swam out into the blue water and turned a somersault, motioning Coral and Tommy to do the same. Then she turned a back flip and so did they. Back on the reef, their parents clapped their hands at the show. Linda pointed to the two children and signalled OK vigorously to their parents, who bowed thanks.

They came to a sand patch, and Linda began to dig beneath the sand. She uncovered a brown oval animal with very short spines, waved the sand away from between the spines, and passed the animal around. "HEART URCHIN," she said. Tommy turned it over and found a tiny white crab—the hitch-hiker Linda had mentioned—nestled between the spines. "GOOD EYES!" Linda praised, and showed the crab to everyone. Coral carefully reburied the urchin in the sand.

As they swam along the reef, Coral found herself looking under every ledge and into every crevice, hoping to find Oliver. In one hole she could see two long spiny antennas moving around. She tapped Linda's arm and pointed at the antennas. "SUPER! A LOBSTER!" Linda took out a piece of fish and held it near the antennas. A few fish tried to nibble at the food, but the lobster fended them off by whipping its antennas around. Slowly it walked toward the food until, with a sudden movement, it jumped onto Linda's hand, grabbed the food with tiny claws, and tried to pull it back into the cave. Linda wouldn't release the fish, though, so the lobster stayed on her hand, munching away. Finally Linda did let go of the bait and the lobster took it back into the crevice, still keeping the greedy little fish away with its talented antennas.

Linda led them to a coral head with what looked like orange feathers sticking out of a crack in it. She reached over and ran her hand along one of the feathers, and her fingers seemed to be stuck! "VELCRO," she said. "TRY IT."

Coral ran her fingers along the feather as Linda had, and, sure enough, the feathers stuck to her fingers. *It DOES seem like Velcro,* she thought as she gently disengaged her hand. Tommy tried it too, and then everyone else. *That crinoid has probably never been so busy!* Coral thought.

83

They came to an open area and Linda motioned the group to settle down on the bottom. She put her gloves on, held out a hot dog, and was immediately mobbed by fish: little cigar-shaped blue-and-yellow wrasses, yellow-and-black striped sergeant-major fish, gentle yellow-and-black French angelfish, and a whole mob of yellowtail snappers. There were so many fish that Linda disappeared in a cloud of them! It didn't take long

85

for the hot dog to be eaten and Linda to reappear, and that was when Coral realized that half of her air was gone. Tommy's was too; they showed Linda their gauges. She signalled "OK" and motioned for them to follow her.

"Now, the mysterious surprise!" Coral thought. It seemed as if they hadn't been in the water very long at all, but the sadness she felt at having to leave—and at not seeing a sign of Oliver—was balanced somewhat by her anticipation of the surprise. She swam along next to Linda, looking ahead, trying to figure out where they were going. She saw the usual coral heads and rocks and fish, and then, as far away as she could see, she saw a spot of white at the side of a coral head. Linda was heading directly toward it.

As they got closer Coral could see that the white thing was a big, bleached-out conch shell. She grabbed Tommy by the arm and pointed, and they dashed ahead of Linda.

"OLIVER-R-R-R!" Coral shouted.

"OLIVER!" Tommy gasped.

And an oh-so-beautiful and familiar head appeared as Oliver emerged from behind the conch shell. "Where've you guys been these days?" he asked casually—but despite how calm he sounded, he was bobbing up and down like crazy.

12   Oliver's Story

Just then Linda and the others caught up with Coral and Tommy. "YOU FOUND OLIVER!" Coral shouted gleefully. "HE WAS THE SURPRISE!"

"OLIVER?" Linda questioned. "ANOTHER OCTOPUS FOR YOU."

That was when Coral realized that Linda didn't know this was the same octopus Linda herself had shown Coral—was it only four days ago? And if Linda was confused, that was nothing to the bewilderment showing on the faces of their parents, right through their face masks!

"THIS IS OUR FRIEND!" Tommy explained. "HE'S THE SAME OCTOPUS."

No one seemed to understand what they meant.

Then Oliver spoke again. "Maybe I can explain," he said, bobbing up and down. Linda's eyes widened and she began to smile. Coral's mother looked around, trying to figure out who was speaking so clearly. Coral's father looked shocked. Muffled sounds were coming from Tommy's mother's regulator as she tried to speak. Tommy's father took his regulator out of his mouth to talk, but only got a mouthful of water. He replaced the regulator quickly.

"*I'm* the one who is speaking," Oliver said, coming to the entrance of his new house and pointing to himself. It was a repeat of what had happened when Coral and Tommy had first

heard Oliver speak. When everyone realized that the octopus was talking, they became very quiet. Only their exhaust bubbles made sounds, and there were plenty of them because everyone was breathing fast from excitement.

"My name is Oliver Octopus," Oliver continued. "As I explained to Coral and Tommy a couple of days ago, I'd tried to talk to humans before but no one ever heard me—that is, until Coral and Tommy did. For a long time I lived under a ledge in the shallow water near here. This lady," Oliver pointed to Linda, "used to come to visit me frequently, and bring others to see me." Oliver bobbed, and bowed to Linda.

"OLIVER, THIS IS OUR FRIEND LINDA. SHE TAUGHT US TO SCUBA DIVE!" Coral told Oliver.

"I'm very pleased to meet you, Linda," Oliver said solemnly.

"I'VE ALWAYS ENJOYED SEEING YOU, OLIVER, AND I'M SORRY WE NEVER HAD THE CHANCE TO TALK BEFORE," Linda said.

"Well, you were always very busy with your students," Oliver told her kindly. "I certainly appreciated the fish you brought on your visits, though."

"BUT THAT DOESN'T MAKE UP FOR ME NOT HAVING THE TIME TO LISTEN. . . ." Linda said, sadly.

Tommy didn't want Linda to feel bad, so he changed the subject. "OLIVER, WHAT HAPPENED? WHY DID YOU MOVE?"

"WE WERE SO WORRIED ABOUT YOU!" Coral added. "AND WE NEVER GOT TO INTRODUCE YOU TO CHELLIE AND JIMMY."

"I had been out hunting that night," Oliver explained, "and arrived home just after sunrise—to find that a big long-spined urchin had taken over my house!"

Coral remembered how she had seen the urchins walking back to shelter early that morning. *Jimmy was right,* she thought, *he said that maybe some animal had found Oliver's house and caused him to move, and it was that sea urchin all along!*

"The urchin had wedged itself into my doorway with its spines," Oliver continued, "and no matter how hard I pulled, I just couldn't get it out! I didn't really think I could move it, and all I *did* do was frighten it into going farther back. But I tried because I knew if I were gone Coral and Tommy would worry. . . . It was very light by then and I was awfully unprotected without my house, so I decided I'd better find another place to spend the day. I grabbed my only precious possession—this conch shell that you gave me," he said looking at Coral and Tommy, "—and went to find some shelter. There wasn't anything nearby so I had to come way out here.

"I knew that Coral and Tommy would be wondering what had happened to me, and I hoped the shell would help them find me—I worried that it might be too deep for them to see, but there was nothing else I could do. As soon as it got dark I visited my old house—and that house-stealing urchin was still there. I must have really frightened it!" He bobbed up and down. "I've missed you two," he concluded.

"AND WE'VE MISSED YOU!" Coral told him, and Tommy nodded in agreement. "WE SEARCHED ALL OVER FOR YOU, AND CHELLIE AND JIMMY HELPED US. BUT WE COULDN'T COME TO WATER THIS DEEP. . . ."

"WE HOPED THAT WE'D BE ABLE TO FIND YOU WHEN WE WERE SCUBA DIVING—AND WE DID!" Tommy added, "WITH LINDA'S HELP."

"OLIVER," Coral's mother began, "IS THERE ANY WAY WE CAN HELP YOU TO GET YOUR OLD HOUSE BACK?"

"Why, thank you, ma'am," Oliver bobbed. "Actually, my new house suits me even better than the old one: it's a little bigger, and I have a much better view from my doorway. And since this house is higher up, it's not likely to get taken over by an urchin! The only *disadvantage* of this house is that Coral and Tommy can't come to visit me here. . . ."

"SURE THEY CAN!" Linda told him. "THEY'RE SUPER DIVERS, AND THEY REALLY KNOW THIS REEF WELL. THEY CAN COME DIVING HERE WITH ME WHENEVER I HAVE STUDENTS—I'LL BE GLAD TO HAVE THEIR HELP!"

"AND WE'LL KEEP AN EYE ON YOUR OLD HOUSE FOR YOU, OLIVER," Coral said. "IF THE URCHIN LEAVES, MAYBE YOU CAN COME BACK—FOR A WHILE, ANYWAY—TO MEET CHELLIE AND JIMMY!"

"It would be a pleasure, Corrie," Oliver replied.

"AND WE'LL BRING YOU SOME MORE FISH TO EAT!" Tommy said.

"That would be *very* nice," Oliver said gravely. "I seem to have developed quite a taste for fish lately. But I still enjoy your company most of all. So please, be sure to visit!"

"YOU BET!" said Tommy.

"AS OFTEN AS WE CAN!" said Coral.

"AND WE'LL COME ALONG TOO, WHENEVER LINDA—AND CORRIE AND TOMMY—LET US!" added Coral's mother.

Linda checked everyone's pressure gauges and signalled that they'd better get back before they ran out of air. The excitement of seeing Oliver had made everyone breathe faster!

"BYE, OLIVER! I'M SO GLAD WE FOUND YOU AGAIN!" Coral said.

"ME TOO! BYE!" Tommy said.

"BYE, OLIVER! IT WAS NICE TO TALK WITH YOU—FINALLY. WE'LL ALL BE SEEING YOU AGAIN SOON!" said Linda.

"BYE, OLIVER! THANKS FOR BEING SUCH A GOOD FRIEND TO OUR KIDS!" said Tommy's father.

Swimming backwards, they waved to Oliver until he was out of sight. Then Linda gestured, "after you," and Coral and

91

Tommy, newly-appointed dive guide assistants, led the way to the dock, brimming with excitement about the days ahead. Some pretty wonderful things can happen to ordinary people, Coral thought—especially when they meet a very special octopus named Oliver.

Spooky Favorites
from Avon Camelot Books!

CREEPS by Tim Schoch
There's a new girl in school—and she's strange! Jeff Moody sets out to prove that Kaybee Keeper is an alien if it's the last thing he does. There's only one problem: what if he's right!
Avon Camelot   **89852-7/$2.50 U.S./$3.25 Can**

THE FIRST ASTROWITCHES
by Marian T. Place Illustrated by Tom O'Sullivan
Our two favorite witches, Witchard and Witcheena, stow away aboard the space shuttle and attempt to locate their parents' lost exploration party. A daring Halloween space adventure.
Avon Camelot   **70056-5/$2.50 U.S./$3.25 Can**

THE WORST WITCH
by Jill Murphy Illustrated by the author
Mildred's first year at Miss Cackle's Academy for Witches is a disaster. But just when she thinks her career is coming to an early end, she surprises everyone—including herself.
Avon Camelot   **60665-8/$1.95**

FRANKENSTEIN'S AUNT by Alan Rune Pettersson
Frankenstein's cigar-chomping no-nonsense aunt returns to the scene of the crime where the monster was created to restore respect for the family name. A hilarious spoof of Frankenstein-Dracula-werewolf stories.
Avon Camelot   **60020-X/$2.50 U.S./$3.25 Can**